Seahorse Stars

Dancing Waves

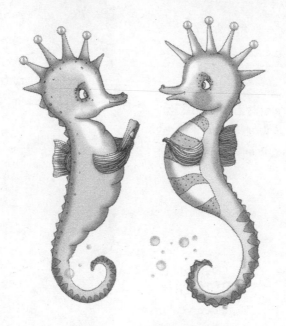

Zuzu Singer

Illustrated by Helen Turner

USBORNE

Meet the Pearlies

Shy but
sweet
CORA is
a pretty
pink seahorse
with pale
pink stripes.

Fun and friendly CAMMIE is
a vivid pink seahorse who dreams
of becoming a Seahorse Star.

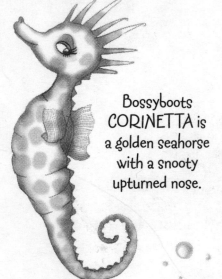

Bossyboots
CORINETTA is
a golden seahorse
with a snooty
upturned nose.

Cammie's
best friend
JESS is
a born
storyteller.
She is a bright
bluey-green.

# of Rainbow Reef

Pale-green
MISS SWISH
is firm but fair
as the elegant
leader of
the Pearlies.

Brainbox BREE
knows all the answers!
She is purple with lovely
lavender fins.

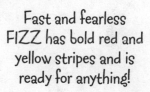

Fast and fearless
FIZZ has bold red and
yellow stripes and is
ready for anything!

Rainbow Reef

Coral Tower

Seahorse City

Eelgrass forest

Palace

Sandy Cove

Pearlie Pavilion

Cammie's House

Pink Sand Plains

Coral Caves

Seahorse Stars is dedicated to every child who
loves to read...including you!

First published in the UK in 2011 by Usborne Publishing Ltd., Usborne
House, 83-85 Saffron Hill, London EC1N 8RT, England.
www.usborne.com

Text copyright © Lee Weatherly, 2011

Illustration copyright © Usborne Publishing Ltd., 2011

A CIP catalogue record for this book is available from the British Library.

JFMAMJJA OND/11 02343/1

ISBN 9781409520306 Printed in Reading, Berkshire, UK.

Chapter One

Cammie Sunbeam and her best friend Jess swam together through the warm waters of Rainbow Reef. All around them were brightly-coloured corals, with white sand below.

"So guess what happens next?" said Jess eagerly. She was a pretty blue-green seahorse, while Cammie herself was a bright, vivid pink.

Cammie held back a sigh. "What?"

"Jessie fights off the shark single-finned!" cried Jess. She darted about in the water, waving her fins. Finally she bobbed in front of Cammie, beaming. "Doesn't that sound like the waviest story ever?"

"Yes, brilliant!" said Cammie. Secretly, though, she was getting rather tired of Jess's stories. Jess had been writing them for weeks now, and although Cammie had liked hearing them at first, they were all the same. A seahorse called *Jessie* faced lots of danger, and overcame it all on her own. But Jess was very proud of her stories, so Cammie pretended to still like them. She'd never want to hurt her best friend's feelings.

To change the subject, Cammie said, "Just think — only two more pearls, and then we'll be Seahorse Stars!" She gazed up at the four gleaming pearls on her crown. She had earned them for learning various skills, and when she'd earned six, she'd finally be a Seahorse Star — a member of the waviest club around!

Seahorse Stars got to go on exciting trips, and do things to help the Reef. Cammie could hardly wait to be one.

But meanwhile, being a Pearlie was the next best thing! Cammie smiled. She and Jess were on their way to their next Pearlies meeting now. It was her favourite time of the week.

Jess nodded as they swam around a clump of eelgrass. "Yes, and I can hardly wait to find out what our next pearl will be for!" She nudged Cammie with her tail. "Hey — maybe it'll be for writing stories! I'd win a pearl easily for that."

Cammie forced a smile. She hoped that Jess would get tired of story-writing soon...or at least start writing stories that weren't all about her! Didn't the heroes of stories ever need best friends, sometimes?

The pink coral walls of the Pearlie Pavilion came into view. Dozens of young seahorses of every colour of the rainbow were heading towards it, all with pearls on their crowns. Cammie's heart quickened with excitement as she watched all the different groups swimming in through the arched doorway. Soon they'd find out about their next pearl!

Entering the Pavilion, Cammie and Jess glided through the water to where their own group, the Dancing Waves, met. The other seahorses were there already, sitting perched on chairs made from seashells.

"I hope we get to do something really exciting for our next pearl!" said Fizz, a sporty seahorse with red and yellow stripes. "Right, Cora?" She nudged another seahorse with her fin.

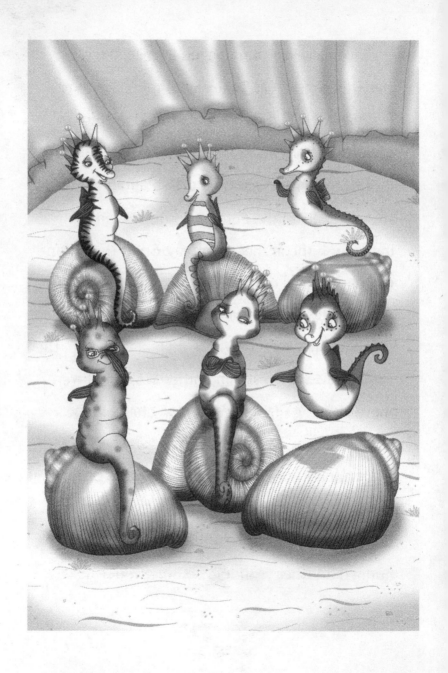

Cora gulped, but managed a smile. "Yes, that would be great," she said weakly. Cammie held back a grin. She knew Cora didn't think it was *great* at all. The pale-pink seahorse was very nervous, and always worried about things being frightening.

Bree, a purple seahorse who loved to read, adjusted her glasses with her fin. "Maybe it'll be something where we can do some research! Wouldn't that be fun?"

Cammie stared at her. She liked Bree a lot, but the brainy seahorse's idea of *fun* was a bit strange at times. "Er...I suppose," she said.

Corinetta tossed her head. She was a bright golden colour, and had an unusually tall crown which she was very proud of. "Well, *I* don't care what we do — so long as we get our next two pearls quickly," she announced in her snooty voice. "I'm ready to be a Seahorse Star now. Being a Pearlie is baby stuff!"

Cammie scowled at her. Trust Corinetta to say something like that! Not for the first time, Cammie thought how much more pleasant the Pearlies would be if only Corinetta wasn't there.

Jess gave an innocent smile, her eyes twinkling. "But we're so glad that you *are* a Pearlie, Corinetta! Why, who would show us how to do things, if you weren't? Like first aid, and camping, and..."

The other seahorses held back a snigger as Corinetta's cheeks turned red. The stuck-up seahorse wasn't as skilled as she liked to think, and had very nearly not got a few of her pearls.

Before Corinetta could reply, Miss Swish,
the Dancing Waves leader, arrived. She was
a tall, pale-green seahorse. Though she could
be very firm at times, Cammie liked her a lot.
Miss Swish knew everything there was to know
about becoming a Seahorse Star!

"Hello, girls!" she said now with a warm smile. "Are you all ready to find out about your next pearl?"

"Yes, Miss Swish!" said everyone together. Cammie sat up straight in her seat, her eyes shining. She could hardly wait!

Miss Swish swam to the front of the Dancing Waves' area. There was a piece of slate there on a coral stand. Picking up a bit of chalk in her tail, Miss Swish wrote *Tidal Team* on the slate in swirling letters. Cammie stared at the words. What did they mean?

"Your fifth pearl is your Tidal Team pearl," said Miss Swish. "Now, who can tell me what that is?"

Cammie wasn't surprised when Bree's fin shot up. The clever seahorse knew almost everything! "We have to show that we can work together as a team," said Bree earnestly.

Miss Swish nodded. "That's right. To earn your fifth pearl, you all have to do something together as a group. For instance, you might write a song together and perform it for everyone, or design and paint a mural. Or you could even plant a seaweed garden, to help the Reef."

Cammie and Jess exchanged an eager look. This pearl sounded like it was going to be lots of fun! "I've got a great idea already," hissed Jess in Cammie's ear. "Just wait until I tell you!"

At the front, Miss Swish was still talking. "Those are just some thoughts — you can decide as a group what you'd like to do. And of course I'll help out if you need it, but mostly I want you to do your project on your own. That way, I can see how well you work together as a team. Now, to earn your pearl, there are two important things to remember."

Miss Swish picked up the chalk again. "One," she said. "Everyone must take part!" She wrote the words down and underlined them. "I need to see that everyone in the group has contributed something. If someone doesn't help, or doesn't do their fair share, then they're letting the rest of the team down."

Cammie couldn't help glancing at Corinetta. If anyone in the Dancing Waves was likely not to pull their weight, it was her!

"Which brings me to the second point," said Miss Swish. "Everyone will be judged the same!" She wrote those words down, too. Looking very serious, she said, "What that means is that for the Tidal Team pearl, the whole team is judged together. So either you'll all get your pearl...or none of you will."

Chapter Two

Cammie felt her eyes grow wide as Miss Swish's words hung in the air. "You mean — even if we do really well, if someone else in our team doesn't, then we won't get our pearl?" she burst out.

Miss Swish smiled. "Don't worry, it's not meant to be scary! If everyone tries their best, then you'll all get your pearls. But I do need to see that everyone's taking an equal part. This pearl is all about teamwork!"

Cammie frowned worriedly. Around her, the other seahorses were exchanging nervous looks. Suddenly this pearl didn't sound quite as much fun as before! But surely it would be okay, Cammie told herself. All they had to do was make sure that they worked together as a team, like Miss Swish said.

"Now, why don't you spend the rest of our time discussing what you might like to do for your team project?" suggested Miss Swish. "You'll be trying for your pearl in just two weeks, so the sooner you decide, the better."

Along with the other girls, Cammie moved her chair so that they were all sitting in a circle.

"I've got a great idea!" burst out Jess. She bounced on her tail. "Why don't we do a play? We could use one of my stories!"

Oh, no! Cammie winced as she saw the other girls making faces. She knew that they were all as tired of Jess's stories as she was. Jess never stopped talking about them!

"Yes, maybe," said Bree, sounding like she was trying to be polite. "But you know what *I* think would be good? A research project about the history of the Pearlies! In fact, I've been doing lots of research about the Pearlies already, just for fun, and—"

Jess's mouth dropped open. "A research project? But—"

"No, here's what *I* think we should do!" broke in Fizz excitedly. She swished her striped

tail. "We should all train for a sporting event —
like the fifty-wave dash! We could have charts
showing how fit we were before we started
training, and how fit we became afterwards,
and—"

"Urgh, that sounds awful!" said Corinetta
with a shudder. She lifted her nose grandly in
the water. "*I* think we should have a beauty
pageant."

"A *beauty pageant*?" repeated Fizz, looking
horrified.

"Yes!" beamed Corinetta. "We could make
trinkets out of shells and things, and decorate
our crowns. Then we could have a contest, to
see which of us is the most beautiful." Her eyes
gleamed. Obviously, she thought that she
would be the winner!

Cammie stared at her. That didn't sound
much like a team activity to her. The other
seahorses didn't seem to think so, either. They
gaped at Corinetta in disbelief. "That is the
most ridiculous—" started Fizz.

"No, listen, we should do a play!"
interrupted Jess. "I just wrote a great story,

didn't I, Cammie?" She nudged her with her fin. "It would be perfect!"

"Um, yes…it's really good," said Cammie feebly.

Bree shook her head. "A research project would be much more interesting. I've already got a big file full of all sorts of facts about the Pearlies that we could use, and—"

"But that means there wouldn't be anything for the rest of us to do," protested Fizz. "We should do a sporting event!"

"A beauty pageant," repeated Corinetta firmly. "It would be *so* wavy…for those of us who have nice, tall crowns, that is." She smiled upwards at her own crown.

"I think we should do something that's for everyone, though," said Cora in a small voice. "Like, I don't know…maybe we could all do a dance, that we make up ourselves?"

The other seahorses hardly even heard her. They were too busy arguing. All except for Corinetta, who scowled at Cora. "That's a terrible idea!" she snapped. "What would we want to do a *dance* for?" Cora gulped, and went silent.

Cammie cleared her throat. "Well, actually, I think a dance sounds..." But no one was listening. Everyone was talking loudly, waving their fins in the water. With a sigh, Cammie gave up.

Finally it was almost time to go home. Miss Swish swam over to them. "Have you decided yet?" she asked. She looked like she was trying not to smile. Cammie had a feeling she'd been listening to them!

"No, not yet," mumbled the girls.

"Well, it might be a good idea for you all to meet up before the next Pearlies meeting," suggested Miss Swish. "I'll give you time to work on your project then, but you'll get more done if you've already decided what you're doing."

The girls all looked at each other. "Where should we meet up?" asked Bree.

"How about my house?" said Cammie quickly, before everyone could start arguing again. "Tomorrow afternoon, after school." She was sure that her parents wouldn't mind.

The girls all agreed. "Good!" said Miss Swish. "I'll look forward to seeing you next week, then...and hearing about what you've decided!"

If we've managed to decide by then, thought Cammie as the seahorses started heading home. She had thought that Corinetta would be the only problem — but *nobody* in the Dancing Waves seemed able to agree!

"I can hardly wait to get started," she overheard an orange seahorse from another group say.

"Me too!" exclaimed her friend. "Cleaning up litter in the Reef — what a great team project!"

They had already chosen! Cammie stared after them in dismay as they glided off. Were the Dancing Waves the only group that still didn't know what they were doing?

Swimming along at Cammie's side, Jess looked cross. "I can't believe that no one liked my idea," she grumbled, batting at a blade of eelgrass with her fin as they passed it. "*You* thought it was good, didn't you, Cammie?"

"Definitely!" said Cammie. "Only..." She trailed off. Jess was so proud of her stories. How would she feel if Cammie told her what she really thought of them?

"Only what?" asked Jess.

"Nothing!" said Cammie quickly. They swam to one side as a school of silvery fish flashed past.

"It's just that…well…" Jess was staring at her. Cammie lost her nerve. "It's just that, they haven't heard your latest story yet! So of course they don't see what a great play it would make."

Argh! Why had she said that? But Jess's eyes were shining. "Of course!" she exclaimed. "I'll bring my story along tomorrow, and read it to everyone. *Then* they'll see! Thanks, Cammie. What a great idea!"

Oh, what had she done? Cammie bit her lip. She knew that the other Dancing Waves weren't going to want to do a play based on Jess's story, no matter what! Everyone was so tired of her stories already. Plus, it was all about Jess — there wouldn't be any good parts for anyone else.

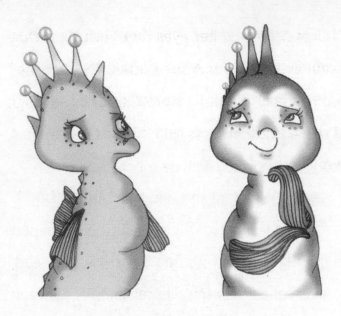

"Jess, maybe — maybe that's not such a
good idea..." she started.

"Why not?" asked Jess in surprise.

Cammie opened her mouth and slowly
closed it again. She *couldn't* tell her friend the
truth – she'd be so hurt! "Just...maybe there
won't be enough time to read the whole thing
out," she said weakly.

Jess narrowed her eyes thoughtfully as they swam along. "Hmm," she said finally. "Maybe you're right." Cammie started to breathe a sigh of relief. But then Jess said, "I'll just *tell* them about the story. That'll be much better!"

Chapter Three

"But—" started Cammie in dismay. It was too late. They had reached the sandy lane where Jess's house was.

"Thanks, Cammie!" said Jess with a big smile. "See you tomorrow!" And she swam off down the lane, humming to herself.

Oh, no! thought Cammie as she turned

slowly down her own lane. What had she done? Now Jess was sure to be upset when the others didn't go along with her idea. And it would all be her fault.

Cammie's house was halfway down the lane, and made of pretty lavender coral built in the shape of a conch shell. When she reached it, her little brother and sister were playing tag in front. "How was Pearlies?" asked Tigg eagerly, darting up to her. Tigg could hardly wait to be a Pearlie, and loved hearing about the meetings.

"Great," said Cammie, trying to smile.

Stripe stared at her. "You don't *look* like it was great," he said. "You look really worried."

"Don't be silly," retorted Tigg. "What has Cammie got to worry about? She has four

pearls already — she's almost a Seahorse Star!"
She sighed. "I wish *I* were you, Cammie."

Cammie smiled sadly. Tigg was still so little.
She had no idea how hard it was sometimes,
being Cammie's age!

Maybe it'll be okay, she tried to tell herself
as she went inside. After all, she hadn't heard
all of Jess's latest story yet. Maybe it was a
really good one, and everyone would love it.

With a groan, she flung herself onto the
sofa. Yes...and maybe rocks could swim!

That night at dinner, Cammie told her parents
about the Dancing Waves coming around the
next day. "Is it okay, Dad?" she asked. Her
father took care of the house during the day.

Her mother was a Rainbow Reef guard, and one of the fastest seahorses in the Reef.

Her father nodded his blue head. "Fine with me!" He stirred the pot of plankton stew that sat on the coral table. "Would you two like some more?" he asked Tigg and Stripe.

Tigg didn't seem to hear him. "Are the Dancing Waves really coming *here*?" she breathed excitedly.

Cammie gave her little sister a sharp look. Oh, no! Tigg was sure to hang about the whole time now, and bother them. "Yes, but we need lots of privacy," she said. "We've got important things to talk about."

Tigg's face fell. "But—"

Cammie's mother, who was a bright pink just like Cammie, gave Tigg's tail a squeeze. "You'll be a Pearlie soon enough," she said gently. "But Cammie's right, Tigg. You need to leave her and her friends alone tomorrow."

"That's not fair!" grumbled Tigg, scowling down at her bowl. "Cammie *always* gets to do the fun things — just because she's older."

Cammie rolled her eyes. She thought that Tigg should try being the older one, for a change! Remembering how she'd had to rescue Tigg from the Deep recently, she wasn't sure what was so "fun" about it.

"You and Stripe can do something special soon, to make up for it," said Dad. He winked at Cammie, and she smiled back in relief. She knew that her father would keep Tigg out of the way. He always understood!

Stripe looked up from his stew in surprise. "But *I* don't need to do anything to make up for it," he pointed out. "I don't care whether I see the Dancing Waves or not."

"Shush!" whispered Tigg, shoving him with her fin. "Or else we won't get to do anything!"

Cammie giggled, and her parents smiled,

too. "Good, I'm glad that's settled," said Cammie's mother, swimming away from the table. "Now, come on, you two — time to get washed, and then off to bed."

As Cammie helped her father with the dishes, he gave her a keen look. "Is everything all right?" he asked.

Cammie sighed. Opening their back door, she threw out the leftover stew. Immediately, a pair of tiny crabs came scuttling up. "Mine!" said one, grabbing up the food. "No, mine!" replied the other, waving its claws. Still arguing, they clattered away again.

"It's just...well, we can't seem to decide what to do for our project," said Cammie finally. She didn't mention the problem with Jess and her story. She knew that not even Dad could help with that!

Her father nodded as he scrubbed the coral bowls out with sand. "Getting everyone to agree is never easy. It sounds like you need a leader."

Cammie blinked in surprise. "But we're supposed to be working as a team."

"Yes, but every team needs someone in charge," said her father. "A good leader can make a big difference. They'll make sure that things are running smoothly, and that everyone's doing what they're best at."

He handed the clean bowls to Cammie. She swam up towards the ceiling, putting them away on their shelf.

"Maybe," she said, thinking of Miss Swish. She knew that the Dancing Waves wouldn't get much done without her. And at school, there was always a leader whenever they had a sports team. Perhaps her father was right.

"Anyway, see what happens tomorrow," he said. "Who knows — maybe it'll go more smoothly than you think!"

Cammie managed a smile. But she had a sinking feeling that whatever happened tomorrow, *smooth* wasn't going to describe it!

Chapter Four

"And then...Jessie fights the shark!" cried Jess. She jetted about the living room so fast that she made currents in the water. "Pow, pow! And the shark swims away! So then Jessie keeps swimming, and she comes to...a giant squid! And—"

"Let me guess, she wins against the squid

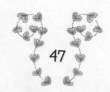

too," muttered Corinetta, staring up at the ceiling. The golden seahorse often made snide comments, but this time everyone seemed to agree with her. Cammie cringed as a faint snigger ran through the room.

Thankfully, Jess was so carried away that she didn't notice. "And then the *squid* swims away!" She spun in the air, waving her fins about. "And then—"

"Um, Jess…I think everyone's got the idea now," said Cammie quickly.

Jess sank down onto the sofa, beaming widely. "Well? What do you all think?" she demanded. "Wouldn't that be *perfect* for a play?"

Silence fell as the Dancing Waves all looked at each other. Cammie held her breath, hoping

that no one would say anything mean. She knew that Jess's stories were a bit one-sided, but she had so much fun writing them!

"I still think we should do a research project," said Bree finally. "It would be really educational, and I've already done most of the work—"

"No! A beauty pageant!" burst out Corinetta.

"We are *not* doing a beauty pageant," said Fizz scornfully. "We should do a sporting event, like I said!"

"Wasn't anyone paying attention?" wailed Jess. "What about my story?"

In no time at all, the room was ringing with raised voices. Cora kept trying to say something, but was drowned out by the others.

Cammie clapped her
fins over her ears.
She could hardly
hear herself think!

"QUIET!" she
shouted. Everyone
stopped talking and
stared at her in
surprise. Cammie felt her
cheeks turn even pinker than normal.
But remembering what her father had said, she
went on. "We won't get anywhere arguing,"
she said. "I think we need a leader — someone
to decide what to do, and be in charge."

Corinetta tossed her head with a smirk.
"*Great* idea!" she said. "I vote that the leader
should be the one with the tallest crown."

"No! I vote that the leader should be Cammie!" burst out Jess excitedly.

Cammie gaped at her. "What? No, wait, I didn't mean me—"

"Yes — Cammie would be perfect!" said Bree. "Everyone who agrees, raise your fin."

All of the Dancing Waves except for Corinetta put their fins up. "I don't think this is fair at all," complained the golden seahorse sulkily.

For once, Cammie agreed with her! "Look, I just meant that someone should be the leader — not me," she said desperately. "I wouldn't be good at all. Can't someone else do it?"

"Too late, O Glorious Leader!" laughed Fizz, patting her on the head. "You're in charge now."

How had *she* ended up as the leader?
Cammie opened and shut her mouth. She had
no idea what to say! Just then Dad swam in,
with a tray full of seaweed biscuits and coral
cake. "How's it going?" he asked, putting the
treats down on the table.

"Great, Mr. Sunbeam," chorused the girls.

When he'd swum out again, Jess grinned and squeezed Cammie's tail. "Okay, leader, it's up to *you* now," she said. "What should we do for our project?"

Looking into her friend's eager eyes, Cammie's heart sank. Oh no — Jess thought that Cammie was going to choose her story! But how could she? If she was the leader, then she had to do what was best for the whole group — and she knew that Jess's story wasn't it.

"Well?" said Bree, adjusting her glasses. "What do you think, Cammie? Whose idea should we choose?"

Cammie hesitated. This was awful! Everyone was watching her, waiting for her to speak. "I…" she started, and then trailed off as she saw Jess's expectant gaze.

"What?" said Fizz.

"I...um..." Cammie stared down at the floor, swishing her tail as she stalled for time. Part of her wanted to choose Jess's idea and make her friend happy. But everyone would be so upset — and she couldn't blame them!

Finally Cammie took a deep breath. "I — I think we should do Cora's idea."

She felt so awful that she could hardly even look at Jess. Out of the corner of her eyes, she saw her friend's face fall in disappointment. Jess stared at Cammie, her eyes hurt.

Most of the other seahorses just looked confused. "When did Cora have an idea?" said Bree blankly.

Cora's cheeks had gone bright pink with surprise. "Yesterday," she said. "I said we should all do a dance that we make up ourselves."

"No!" burst out Corinetta. "Who wants to do a *dance*? What a stupid idea!" Cammie's

eyes widened in surprise. Even if Corinetta
didn't want to do a dance, why did she sound
so upset about it?

"Actually, you know what...it's not bad!"
said Fizz. "If we're not doing a sporting event,
then I'd rather do a dance than anything else.
At least it's something active — and we can put
some really wavy moves in!" Swimming over to
Cora, she squeezed her tail. "Good one, Cora!"

Cora beamed with pride. Bree made a face.
"A dance? Oh, I suppose..." she began
reluctantly.

Remembering what Bree had wanted to do,
all at once Cammie gasped. "Wait, I've got a
great idea!" she said. "Dances tell a story
sometimes, don't they? So we could—"

"We could use my story!" interrupted Jess,

her eyes shining. "Cammie, you're right, that's perfect! *Jessie Meets the Shark* could be a dance."

Oh, no! Cammie tried to smile. "No, um... I meant, we could do a dance showing the history of the Pearlies," she said weakly. "Bree already knows all about it, so..."

Fizz's face lit up. "Hey, that *is* perfect!"

Bree nodded, looking pleased. "It would be something really different."

Suddenly Bree, Cora and Fizz were all up and talking excitedly, swapping ideas. Still looking cross, Corinetta turned away, sitting on the sofa apart from everyone.

Cammie found herself alone with Jess. "Listen, um...I'm really sorry..." she started.

Jess looked like she was trying not to cry.

"*I* don't care," she said stiffly. "You can do whatever you like. You're the leader, after all!"

Cammie winced. "Oh, Jess, don't—"

But she was talking to thin water. Jess ignored Cammie and plunked herself on the opposite end of the sofa from Corinetta. The two of them sat scowling.

Cammie stared at Jess, feeling stung. She knew how hurt her friend must be — but she had been the one to suggest Cammie as the leader in the first place! Had Jess only said that because she thought Cammie would choose her idea?

Suddenly Cammie felt hurt, too. Maybe Jess didn't *really* think that she'd be a good leader at all.

Well, I'm going to prove her wrong, she thought, curling her tail up tightly. *I'm going to be the very best leader there is, so that we all get our pearls!*

Chapter Five

Cammie cleared her throat. "Um — all right, everyone!" she called. "Why don't we start planning now? There's lots to decide!"

As the seahorses munched seaweed biscuits and coral cake, Cammie got out a piece of eelgrass to write things down on. "Cora, why don't you and Fizz be in charge of making up the dance and teaching it to the rest of us?" she asked. Her father had said that a good leader would make sure everyone was doing what they were best at. And she knew that Cora and Fizz were both really good dancers!

Cora glowed. "I'd love to!"

Fizz looked happy, too. "Wavy! I know lots of great moves we can put in." She gave a shimmy in the water, twirling her tail.

Everyone laughed — apart from Jess and Corinetta, who still sat glowering. Cammie tried to ignore them. She wasn't going to let the way Jess was acting get to her.

"Great!" she said, writing Cora and Fizz's names down. "And Bree, you can tell them all about the history of the Pearlies, so that they can put it in the dance." Bree nodded.

"Let's see, what else is there to do?" mused Cammie, tapping her coral pen.

"We'll need music," pointed out Fizz.

Immediately, Cammie knew who would be perfect for that...but would she do it? She looked across at Jess. "Um...would you like to be in charge of the music?"

"I'm not very musical," said Jess coolly.

Cammie held back a groan. "I meant, in

charge of finding music," she said. "You've got loads of coral discs. I bet you could find something really good for us to dance to."

"Mm. S'pose," muttered Jess, looking away.

Cammie gritted her teeth and wrote down Jess's name. "And Corinetta, why don't you be in charge of costumes?" she suggested.

Remembering how the golden seahorse had wanted to do a beauty pageant, Cammie thought that Corinetta would really enjoy this...but she just pulled a face. "Yes, all right," she said stiffly.

At least most of the others seemed excited. Cora, Fizz and Bree quickly arranged that they'd meet up in a few days to plan the dance together. "Then we can start teaching it to you at the next Pearlies meeting," said Cora, bobbing up and down in the water. "It's going to be *so* great, all of us dancing together! I bet we'll have the best project of anyone — none of the other groups will have anything like this!"

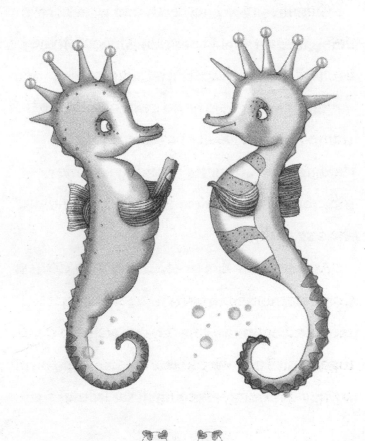

Cammie saw Corinetta flush and duck her head down. She gazed at her in surprise. Was Corinetta all right? But when the golden seahorse looked up again, she was scowling.

"Whatever. I need to go home now," she announced, grabbing her things. And without waiting for an answer, she jetted from the room and out the door, leaving a swirl of bubbles behind her.

The other seahorses all stared at each other in surprise. "Wow, I wonder what's wrong with *her*?" said Bree.

Fizz lifted her fins in a shrug. "Oh, she's just upset that no one wanted to do a beauty pageant. You know what she's like!"

Cammie hesitated. Somehow, it seemed to her that Corinetta might be upset, rather than

just stroppy. But then she remembered how cross Corinetta had looked when she dashed off, and decided that Fizz was probably right.

Cora smiled shyly at Cammie. "Anyway, thanks for choosing my idea," she said. "I was so surprised!"

"Um...that's okay," said Cammie, feeling awkward. She was very aware of Jess sitting right there, watching her!

"It was definitely the right choice, Cammie," said Bree warmly. "No one else would have had much to do on the research project, and only Fizz is really good at sport, and Jess's story—" She broke off suddenly.

"What about my story?" said Jess with a frown.

Bree looked uncomfortable. "Nothing," she

said. "It's just—" She took a deep breath. "Well, all of your stories are the same, aren't they?"

Jess blinked. "They...they are?"

Bree nodded. "Yes, they're always about Jessie getting out of trouble, single-finned. It gets sort of predictable, after a while. Plus there's only one main role — Jessie!"

Jess looked slowly around her, her cheeks reddening. "You mean...nobody likes my stories?" she said in a small voice.

"The first couple that you wrote were

good," said Fizz. "But then they got a bit..."
She made a face.

"Anyway, Jess, I bet you'll do a great job
with the music!" put in Cora quickly. "Do you
have any ideas?"

At first Cammie thought Jess wasn't going
to answer. Then she gave a strained smile.
"Not yet," she said. "But I'll think about it,
and bring some coral discs with me to the
next Pearlies meeting."

Soon it was time for everyone to go home.
Fizz, Bree and Cora all left together, chattering
happily about the project. Jess started to
follow after them. "Jess, wait!" Cammie burst
out. She hated arguing with her best friend.

Jess hesitated by the doorway, not looking
at her. "What?" she said.

Cammie swam over. "I'm really sorry about not choosing your idea," she said again. "It's just that—"

"Just that you didn't like it after all," interrupted Jess. She whirled around to face Cammie. "You know, you could have told me earlier! I kept asking and asking you what you thought."

Cammie gulped, taken aback by the angry look on Jess's face. "But – I didn't want to hurt your feelings—"

"Yes, and so you let me act out my story in front of everyone, when you *knew* nobody would like it!" cried Jess. "Thanks a lot, Cammie. I wouldn't have done that to you!" And with that, Jess spun away and zoomed out the door.

Cammie stared after her, stunned. So that was what she got for trying to spare Jess's feelings! But then guilt washed over her. Jess was right. She should have been honest with her, instead of letting her act her story out in front of the whole group. Poor Jess! She must feel so humiliated now.

I'll apologize to her at school tomorrow, thought Cammie.

Just then her father swam into the lounge, and started clearing things away. "How did it go?" he asked cheerfully.

Cammie sighed, not really wanting to talk about it. "Oh...all right, I guess." She took a deep breath. "You remember what you said, about how we needed a leader? Well, we've got one now!"

"Oh, good! Who?" Then her father saw the look on her face, and smiled. "Oh, I see — it's you, isn't it?"

Cammie nodded grimly.

"Don't worry, I'm sure you'll do a great job," he said, patting her fin. "It's not always easy being a leader, but I know you've got what it takes."

Cammie tried to smile. "Thanks, Dad." She hoped that her father was right...but then she thought again of Corinetta, and Jess, and somehow she wasn't sure at all. Everything seemed to be going wrong already — and she'd only just started!

Chapter Six

Though Cammie apologized to Jess at school the next day, her best friend remained cool with her. They still hadn't made up by the time the next Pearlies meeting came around, so that Cammie swam to the Pearlie Pavilion alone, feeling glum.

Ahead of her, she saw Corinetta going to

the Pavilion, too. *Maybe I should go and talk to her,* thought Cammie, remembering how upset Corinetta had seemed the other day. She put on a burst of speed, but Corinetta was too far away to catch up. The golden seahorse glided into the Pavilion ahead of Cammie, her tail swishing back and forth.

When Cammie arrived at the Dancing Waves' area, Corinetta had already sat down. Jess was there, too, chatting with the others. "Hello, leader!" said Fizz cheerfully. "We've just been talking to Jess about the music for our dance. She's got some wavy ideas!"

"Great!" said Cammie. She looked at Jess hopefully, but her friend seemed determined not to catch her eye. With a sigh, Cammie sat down in the only empty seat, next to Corinetta.

The golden seahorse didn't look at her, either. She was flipping through a seahorse magazine, and acted as if Cammie wasn't even there.

"Hello, girls!" said Miss Swish as she arrived. "Have you decided on your project yet?"

Everyone glanced at Cammie. Suddenly she realized that as the leader, they expected her to explain. "Yes, we're going to do a dance about the history of the Pearlies," she said.

"What a good idea!" exclaimed Miss Swish warmly. Her eyes twinkled. "Did you have a difficult time deciding?"

"It was hopeless," confessed Bree with a grin. "But then we voted for Cammie to be our leader, and she decided for us!"

Miss Swish nodded. "It sounds like you're learning a lot about working in a team," she said. "Good for you, Cammie. It's not always easy being the leader, is it?"

"Er...no, not really," said Cammie shyly, glancing at Jess. Her best friend was gazing off in the other direction, not looking at her.

"Well, I'll give you the rest of our time today to work on your dance," said Miss Swish with a smile. "But first, I've got some exciting news! When you try for your Tidal Team pearl next week, the other Pearlie groups will be trying for theirs at the same time. So each group is going to share its project with the others."

"You mean — all the other Pearlies will be watching when we do our dance?" asked Cammie. Her fins went cold at the thought. There were about a hundred Pearlies!

Miss Swish nodded. "Yes, we thought it would be fun to see what everyone's been doing. Now then, the rest of this time is yours to practise. I'll leave you in charge, Cammie, while I go and chat with the White Pearls' leader for a moment."

"Oh, no — everyone will be watching us!" moaned Cora the moment Miss Swish was gone. "I — I'm feeling all funny in my tummy, just thinking about it." For a change, no one teased Cora for being nervous. They all looked as if they felt the same way!

Cammie tried to push her own fears aside. "It'll be fine," she reassured the group. "We've got a really wavy dance, and I just know that everyone will love it! Why — why, it would be a shame if we *didn't* have an audience. Our dance is going to be the very best team project there is!" Cammie's voice rose as she got a bit carried away, waving her fins about.

Fizz started to smile. "You haven't even *seen* the dance yet," she pointed out.

"All right — so show it to me!" said Cammie with a laugh. "Come on, Cora and Fizz. What do we do?"

"I brought some music along," said Jess, bringing out her portable coral disc player. She put one on, and a song by a popular seahorse band started to play. The bright, cheerful music pulsed through the water.

Fizz grinned, swaying in time to it. "Perfect!" she said. "Okay, everyone come up front, and Cora and I will start teaching you the dance."

Cammie swam up front with the others. Then she noticed that Corinetta was still sitting on her seashell chair. "You too, Corinetta," she called.

The golden seahorse sniffed. "You know, I *really* think that doing the costumes is a big enough job for one seahorse," she said snootily. "I shouldn't have to be part of the dance, too."

"What?" said Cammie in surprise. "But everyone's doing other jobs, not just you!"

"Yes, but I've really got too much to do," said Corinetta. She held up the seahorse magazine she had been looking through.

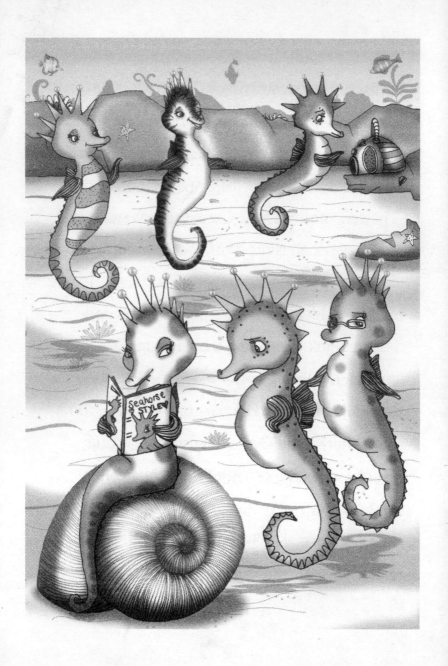

"I'm busy trying to find the perfect costumes for us. It's *not* easy."

"But they shouldn't be anything fancy — they just need to look like Pearlie outfits," said Bree in surprise. "So it'll just be different kinds of pearls, plus the Pearlies used to wear a sash, once."

Corinetta looked flustered. "Yes, well…I'll still be too busy to dance," she muttered.

"But you have to!" protested Cammie. "We all have to take part, or else we won't get our pearl."

Corinetta bit her lip. Finally she burst out, "Well, anyway, I can't right now — I've got a sprained tail."

"*What*?" Cammie stared at her, remembering how Corinetta had glided so quickly ahead of her as they'd gone into the Pearlie Pavilion. There had been nothing wrong with her tail then. "Corinetta, your tail's fine!"

"It is not. It's very sore," said Corinetta, glaring at her. "And I'm *not* going to dance on it and hurt myself. You can't make me!" Opening her magazine again, she buried her snout in it.

Oh, great! thought Cammie. *What now?* Suddenly she noticed that Jess had a funny expression on her face as she gazed at the golden seahorse. But before she could wonder what it meant, Fizz was dragging her aside.

"Cammie, you can't let her get away with this!" she hissed from behind her striped fin. "She's just still sulking because no one liked her idea."

Bree nodded, following after them. Her eyes looked worried behind her glasses. "She's going to ruin it for everyone, if she won't dance. We won't get our pearls!"

Cammie's thoughts were spinning about like a whirlpool. What was she going to do if Corinetta really refused to take part? She couldn't *make* her dance! Finally she took a deep breath. "Let's — let's just start learning the dance without her," she said. "I'm sure she'll come around soon."

"I doubt it," muttered Fizz darkly. But she didn't argue further.

As everyone started moving into place, Jess pulled Cammie to one side too. There was a sheepish expression on her face. "Um...I've been acting just as bad as Corinetta, haven't I?" she said in a low voice.

Cammie smiled as relief rushed through her. "No, not *that* bad," she assured her friend.

Jess blew out a breath. "Oh, Cammie, I'm really sorry! I should have accepted your apology, and not kept sulking. I just...felt so embarrassed, knowing that no one liked my stories." She hung her head.

"No, you were right!" burst out Cammie.
"Jess, I should have told you the truth."

Jess tried to smile. "I wouldn't have liked
hearing it very much."

"No, but I should have anyway," said

Cammie earnestly. "Best friends should always be honest with each other."

"Are we still best friends, then?" said Jess, her eyes hopeful.

"Of course!" cried Cammie, bobbing in the water. "Oh, Jess, I've really missed you." The two seahorses squeezed tails tightly.

"Are you two coming?" called Fizz.

"Coming!" said Cammie with a grin. Suddenly the trouble with Corinetta didn't seem as important any more. She had her best friend back — and that was all that mattered!

Chapter Seven

But as the days passed, Cammie became more and more worried. The dance that Cora and Fizz had put together was lots of fun, and the Dancing Waves were practising it together at Cammie's house almost every day. Yet although Corinetta came to every practice session, she wouldn't dance. She just sat with her nose stuck in a magazine, saying that she was too busy planning their costumes...or that her tail still hurt...or a dozen other excuses. No matter what Cammie did or said, the golden seahorse wouldn't budge.

"Corinetta, you *have* to dance," said Cammie desperately after several days of this. "Or else none of us will get our pearls."

To Cammie's surprise, Corinetta looked almost ashamed for a moment — and then she tossed her head and gave her usual unpleasant smirk. "So? This stupid dance wasn't *my* idea."

Cammie's jaw dropped. "But — even if you don't care about the rest of us, don't you care if *you* don't get your pearl?"

Watching closely, Cammie thought that the other seahorse's jaw trembled. Then Corinetta looked quickly away. "Um...I have to go now," she muttered. Grabbing up her things, she swished out the door before Cammie could react.

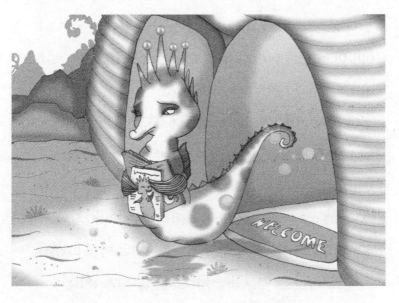

"Cammie, you *have* to do something," said Fizz hotly the moment she'd left. "We'll be trying for our pearl in just a few days now. None of us will get them unless Corinetta dances, too!"

"I'm trying!" said Cammie, feeling close to tears. "I don't know what's wrong with her. She doesn't seem to care if we get our pearls or not."

"Maybe you should tell Miss Swish what's happening," put in Cora, her large eyes looking even wider than normal.

Bree nodded. "I think so, too. Otherwise Corinetta's going to ruin it for the rest of us."

Cammie winced. Telling Miss Swish was the last thing she wanted to do! How could she admit that she was doing such an awful job as the leader? "No, I'll — I'll sort it," she said weakly. "It'll be okay, I promise!"

As the others left, Jess gave Cammie a sympathetic look. "This really isn't turning out to be easy, is it?"

Picking up the last seaweed biscuit, Cammie nibbled dully at it. "No," she admitted. She tried to smile at her friend. "Thanks a lot for suggesting me as leader!"

Jess gave a rueful smile in return. "Sorry! So what are you going to do about Corinetta?"

Cammie sighed. Realizing that she wasn't hungry after all, she put the biscuit down again. "I don't know," she admitted. "I really don't know!"

To make matters worse, the problem with Corinetta wasn't the only thing that was going wrong. The more they practised their dance, the more certain Cammie was that something was missing from it...but she couldn't quite put her fin on what it was.

That night Cammie lay on her bed of soft seaweed, gazing up at the shell mural on her bedroom ceiling as she thought. The dance told the history of the Pearlies – all about how they were first formed by a wise seahorse named Mia, and how it had grown from a tiny group

to one of the most popular clubs in Rainbow
Reef.

But somehow, even though Fizz and Cora
had worked out some great moves for them all
to do, the story part of the dance didn't seem
very clear to Cammie. She wondered if anyone
watching it would even know what they were
trying to say. Then she sighed. Not that it really
mattered — if Corinetta still kept refusing to
dance, then none of them were going to get
their pearls anyway!

Cammie's mother swam in. "It's time you
were asleep now," she chided, perching on the
bed. She smoothed her pink fin over Cammie's
forehead. "Is everything all right?"

Cammie hesitated. She hadn't told her
parents about the trouble she was having, but

now somehow it all came out. She explained about Corinetta. "I don't know what to do," she finished up. "If Corinetta won't dance…"

Her mother looked thoughtful. "How strange," she said. "From what you've said, Corinetta's really eager to be a Seahorse Star.

I wonder if there's a problem that you don't know about?"

"A problem?" repeated Cammie with a frown. Suddenly she remembered how Corinetta's jaw had seemed to tremble that afternoon, as if she was upset.

Her mother nodded. "I don't think that she'd be risking her fifth pearl unless something was really wrong. But you don't need to deal with this on your own, sweetie. Would you like me to speak to Miss Swish for you?"

Slowly, Cammie shook her head. "No, not yet. We've got another practice tomorrow afternoon. I'll try talking to Corinetta again then."

"All right," said Mum finally. "But let me know if you change your mind and want some help. Now, time for sleep." Kissing Cammie's cheek, she glided from the room, shutting the door behind her.

Cammie nestled down onto her bed, still thinking hard. Her mother was right, she just knew it. Somehow, she had to find out what was wrong with Corinetta. All of their pearls depended on it!

The next afternoon, Corinetta swam through Cammie's front door as if nothing had happened. "I've got our costumes here," she said cheerfully, holding up a box made from a seashell. "They're *so* wavy! I've done sashes for everyone, and I've got some black pearls from when the Pearlies used them instead of white ones, and—"

The other seahorses were there already.
They glowered at her. "Who cares?" muttered
Fizz under her breath. "If you won't dance,
none of us will get our pearls anyway!"

Cammie swam quickly over to Corinetta.
"Listen, um...is everything all right?" she asked
in a low voice.

Corinetta stiffened. "Everything's fine. Why?"

Glancing over her shoulder at the others, Cammie took her to one side. "Corinetta, I *know* that you want to get your fifth pearl. So why won't you dance? Is there a problem, or maybe something that's bothering you?"

For a moment the golden seahorse looked uncertain, and Cammie's heart quickened. Then Corinetta seemed to recover herself. "As if I'd tell *you*," she said with a sneer.

"So there *is* something wrong," cried Cammie. "Corinetta, you have to tell me! Maybe I can help."

"Believe me, you can't," muttered Corinetta. Then her cheeks went pink. "I — I mean — there's nothing's wrong! Just leave me alone, Cammie."

To Cammie's alarm, Corinetta looked close to tears. "What *is* it?" she insisted. She lay her fin on Corinetta's. "Tell me what's wrong... please?"

Corinetta jerked away. Her face went bright red, as if she was about to explode. "*I can't dance!*" she burst out finally. "All right? That's what's wrong! I can't dance!"

Chapter Eight

Cammie's jaw fell open in surprise. Behind her, the other seahorses were gaping, too. "You — you can't dance?" she repeated.

"No!" Corinetta wiped her eyes. "I never *have* been able to. I — I can't follow the moves, and I'm clumsy, and it's just awful! If I have to dance in front of everyone, I'll be a laughing stock."

"But Corinetta, it doesn't matter!" cried Cammie. "Miss Swish said that as long as you tried your best, we'd all get our pearls. So all you have to do is try. It doesn't matter if you're any good or not."

"It matters to *me*," wailed Corinetta. "I don't want to look stupid in front of everyone!

I had to do a dance recital once when I was younger, and — and everyone laughed at me." She hung her head. "I never want to go through that again, not ever."

Cammie bit her lip. Suddenly she felt really sorry for Corinetta. It didn't sound like she'd been having much fun, either, these last few days.

The others looked sympathetic, too... especially Jess. "I — I know how you feel," she said haltingly. "It's awful when you think you've made a fool of yourself." Cammie knew that Jess was thinking of her stories. She winced, wishing again that she'd told her friend the truth sooner.

Bree tapped her chin. "Well, you have to do *something,* Corinetta," she pointed out.

"Or else none of us will get our pearls."

"But what?" choked out Corinetta. She sniffed. "I — I don't want to hold any of you back, but I *can't* dance. I really can't!"

Suddenly Cammie remembered what her father had said, about making sure that everyone was doing what they were best at. Looking from Corinetta to Jess and back again, an idea started to come to her. Jess was good at writing, even if everyone had got tired of her stories about *Jessie*. And Corinetta loved showing off and being the centre of attention.

Of course! thought Cammie as excitement sizzled through her. It would solve everything — including the problem with the dance! She turned quickly to the others. "You know, I've been thinking — I don't think that the dance is quite right the way it is," she said. "It's sort of hard to follow the story."

Fizz looked stung. "Well, it's not easy to tell a story with only a dance," she protested.

Cora nodded. "We did our best, Cammie — we really did!"

"Yes, and it's great!" Cammie assured them. "But...I just think it needs something else."

"Like what?" asked Bree, blinking behind her glasses.

"A narrator!" said Cammie. "Someone to explain what's going on, and tell the story while the rest of us dance it." She spun on her tail to face Corinetta and Jess. "Jess, *you* could write the narrator's part — and Corinetta, you could be the narrator!"

There was a surprised silence, and then everyone burst out talking at once. "Cammie, that's a brilliant idea!" cried Jess, her eyes gleaming. "I'd love to!"

"Ooh, yes!" exclaimed Corinetta. "I'd be perfect as the narrator. It should be a really *distinguished* seahorse, after all." She tossed her head, and Cammie held back a smile. Corinetta must be feeling less worried now — she was back to her old snooty self again already!

By the next practice, Jess had written the narrator's part and Corinetta had begun to memorize it. She swished about grandly as the others danced, saying her lines very dramatically.

"Once there was a wise seahorse called Mia," she said. Bree swam into place, doing the graceful moves that Cora and Fizz had planned.

"And one day Mia decided that there should be a club for young seahorses, called…" Corinetta widened her eyes. *Seahorse Stars!*"

Cammie danced with the others, joining tails and spinning in a circle as Corinetta went on. "But you couldn't be a Seahorse Star

immediately. First you had to be a Pearlie, and learn lots of skills…"

Cammie smiled as the dance went on, with her and the others all waving their fins and doing somersaults in the water. The words that Jess had written were making a big difference. Suddenly the dance made much more sense than before!

"Brilliant!" exclaimed Fizz as they finished. "Cammie, you were right — it's so much better than it was."

"Yes, thanks to my delivery," smirked Corinetta, looking smug.

"And *your* writing," laughed Bree, nudging Jess with her tail. "It's really good, Jess!" The others eagerly agreed. Cammie felt warm inside as she saw her friend beam in delight. She was so glad that she'd thought of asking Jess to write the narrator's part! Now maybe she wouldn't feel quite so awful about what had happened with her story.

Corinetta scowled. "Well, yes, the words aren't bad. But it's all in how you *say* them, really, and—"

Cammie grinned, not even minding Corinetta's bragging for once. "Come on, everyone, let's practise it again," she broke in. "We've only got two days left now before we try for our pearl!"

Chapter Nine

When the time for the next Pearlies meeting
came, Cammie felt bubbly with excitement.
She could hardly wait to try for their fifth pearl.
Miss Swish was sure to be impressed — the
Dancing Waves had really come together as
a team!

As she and Jess swam into the Pearlie

Pavilion, they saw that the large space at its centre was filled with rows and rows of seashell chairs. Most of them were filled already with young seahorses. Cammie slowed slightly, staring. There were even more Pearlies than she had thought!

Miss Swish greeted them warmly. "Hello, girls! We're all sitting over here today, so that we can watch the other groups." She guided Cammie and Jess to where the other Dancing Waves were sitting.

Cammie gulped as they took a seat. *How could she have forgotten about performing in front of everyone?* All at once her tail felt cold.

"Are you all right?" whispered Bree, leaning towards her. "You look sort of...green."

Cammie nodded quickly. She couldn't let

her friends know how scared she was — not when she was supposed to be the leader! "Fine," she muttered.

One by one, each of the groups got up and did their team activity. Cammie sat in a nervous daze, hardly taking it in. "So that was how we worked as a team, and cleaned up all the litter in Rainbow Reef," finished a pretty blue seahorse, holding up a chart.

Everyone applauded. The White Pearls' group leader swam forward, looking pleased. "Very well done, Sapphire! I'm pleased to say that you've all earned your pearls." The applause turned to cheers as she put a fifth pearl on each seahorse's crown. The White Pearls returned to their seats, looking flushed and excited.

Cammie started as Jess nudged her. "It's
our turn!" she hissed.

All at once Cammie's mouth felt dry as
sand. "I – um…"

The other Dancing Waves were all staring at
her. "*Cammie!* Come on, what are you waiting
for?" insisted Jess.

"You — you lot go on," said Cammie faintly. She couldn't perform in front of all of these seahorses, she just couldn't!

"*What?*" burst out Bree and Fizz at the same time.

"But we can't do it without you!" cried Cora. "We won't get our pearls."

"I know, but — but I can't..." Cammie wanted so much to move, but she felt frozen. Was *she* going to be the reason that no one got their pearl now? Tears prickled at her eyes.

"Oh, I see — you're scared!" drawled Corinetta in a mean voice. "You know, I really thought you had more sand than this, Cammie. Well, come on, everyone. At least let's show Miss Swish that *we're* not cry-crabs!"

Anger flashed through Cammie. Her chin

jerked up as she glared at Corinetta. "I am *not*
a cry-crab! I just—"

"You're just what? Just too scared to dance,
that's all!" sneered Corinetta. The other
Dancing Waves remained silent, watching them
both with wide eyes.

"Girls, is there a problem?" asked Miss
Swish, swimming over.

"No!" burst out Cammie, still angry. "I mean
— no, Miss Swish." She pushed past the others.
"I am *not* too scared," she muttered between
gritted teeth. "Now come on, let's go!"

They swam up to the front. Jess had
brought her coral disc player with her. She hit
the *play* button, and the music began. Too
cross to feel nervous any more, Cammie
plunged into the dance as Corinetta began to

speak. "Once, there was a wise seahorse called Mia…"

As the story went on, the Dancing Waves tied blue sashes around their middles to show what the Pearlies used to wear. They all twirled in a circle, spinning on their tails. Dimly, Cammie realized that the audience was swaying

to the music. Everyone was smiling and enjoying themselves. Their dance was a success!

Finally the Dancing Waves all linked tails. "And that's the history of the Pearlies!" finished up Corinetta triumphantly. She even did a little dance move of her own as the music ended.

The audience burst into applause. Cammie blinked as it suddenly hit her that she'd just been dancing in front of a hundred Pearlies! But somehow, it had been okay. It had even been fun.

"Well done, girls!" Miss Swish came swimming over to them. "I can see that you've worked well together as a team."

Cammie nodded, still feeling dazed. "Yes, we — we all did something. Jess wrote the story and found the music, and Bree did the research and helped Fizz and Cora put the dance together, and Corinetta made the costumes—"

"And Cammie was our leader — the worst job of all!" grinned Fizz, nudging her.

Miss Swish laughed. "Well, I'm very pleased to say that you've each earned your pearl," she said. Producing six gleaming pearls, she put one on each of the Dancing Waves' crowns. The audience cheered.

Cammie's heart swelled as she received the shiny new pearl on her crown. They had done it! There had been so many times over the last two weeks when she'd really doubted that they could. But they each had their fifth pearl!

After all the Pearlie groups had finished, the group leaders served seaweed munchies and sandy sweets. The seahorses all mingled together, chatting and laughing. Spotting Corinetta in the crowd, Cammie swam over to her.

"Listen, um...I just wanted to say thanks," she said awkwardly. "If it wasn't for you getting me angry, then we might not have got our pearls after all."

For a moment Corinetta seemed lost for words. "That's okay," she said finally. "And besides, um...you helped me, too, you know. So...thanks for that."

The two seahorses regarded each other shyly. Why, there was a part of Corinetta that was really okay, realized Cammie suddenly. It was just a shame that she didn't show it more!

"There you two are," cried Fizz as she and the other Dancing Waves all came swimming up.

"Yes, we've come to celebrate with you!" laughed Bree.

"Can you believe it?" said Jess excitedly, her eyes gleaming. "We only have one more pearl to go, and then we'll be—"

"*Seahorse Stars!*" Cammie cried with the others.

They all spun on their tails, churning the water around them. Even as she spun, Cammie

could sense her fifth pearl, gleaming in the
light. Happiness burst through her. She
could hardly wait to try for her sixth pearl!

With any luck...she'd soon be a
Seahorse Star.

The End

Dive in with Cammie and her friends and
collect every splash-tastic tale in

Seahorse Stars!

The First Pearl   ISBN 9781409520245

Cammie is thrilled to be a member of the Pearlies
— the waviest club in Rainbow Reef. Her first task
is to go camping. Will she keep her cool, or
is she in too deep?

First-Aid Friends   ISBN 9781409520252

When Cammie's best friend shows a natural talent for
first-aid, Cammie gets competitive...and soon it's their
friendship that needs patching up!

The Lost Lagoon   ISBN 9781409520269

Cammie is confused by compasses and lost when
it comes to maps, so earning her Wave Wanderer
pearl is proving tricky. When stuck-up Corinetta
offers to help, Cammie is grateful. But can
Corinetta be trusted?

Danger in the Deep   ISBN 9781409520276

Cammie loves studying for her Sea Safety pearl
and learning about the dangers of the Deep. So when
her little sister disappears, it's up to Cammie
to rescue her...

Dancing Waves   ISBN 9781409520306

All the seahorses must work together if they are
to earn their Tidal Team pearl...and they've chosen
Cammie as their team leader. Can she stop them
squabbling and help them come out on top?

The Rainbow Queen   ISBN 9781409520313

To get her last Proficiency Pearl, Cammie must do
a good deed in Rainbow Reef...and then she will be a
Seahorse Star! But when Cammie begins her task, she
realizes the Reef is in danger, and she must ask
the Queen for help.

For more wonderfully wavy reads
check out
www.fiction.usborne.com